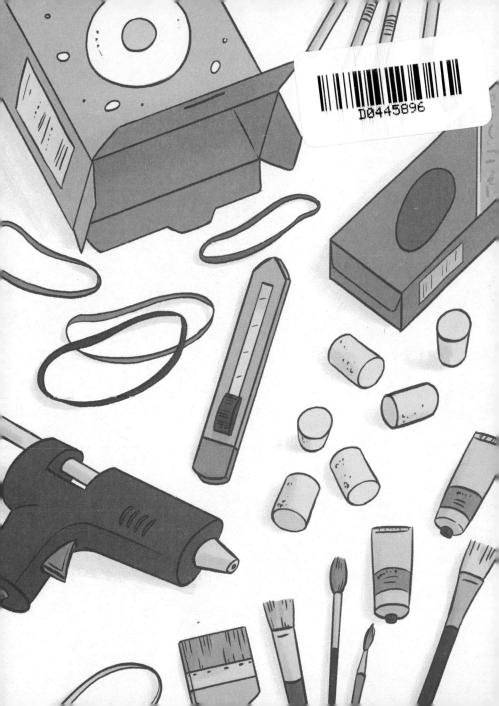

Craft ILY EVER AFTER

- - Making the Band - -

By Martha Maker   **Illustrated by Xindi Yan**

LITTLE SIMON

New York London Toronto Sydney New Delhi

LITTLE SIMON
An imprint of Simon & Schuster Children's Publishing Division
1230 Avenue of the Americas, New York, New York 10020
First Little Simon paperback edition March 2018
Copyright © 2018 by Simon & Schuster, Inc.
All rights reserved, including the right of reproduction in whole or in part in any form.
LITTLE SIMON is a registered trademark of Simon & Schuster, Inc., and associated colophon is
a trademark of Simon & Schuster, Inc.
For information about special discounts for bulk purchases, please contact Simon & Schuster
Special Sales at 1-866-506-1949 or business@simonandschuster.com.
The Simon & Schuster Speakers Bureau can bring authors to your live event. For
more information or to book an event contact the Simon & Schuster Speakers Bureau
at 1-866-248-3049 or visit our website at www.simonspeakers.com.
Designed by Laura Roode.
The text of this book was set in Caecilia.
Manufactured in the United States of America 0218 MTN
2 4 6 8 10 9 7 5 3 1
Cataloging-in-Publication Data is available for this title from the Library of Congress.
ISBN 978-1-5344-0911-8 (hc)
ISBN 978-1-5344-0910-1 (pbk)
ISBN 978-1-5344-0912-5 (eBook)

CONTENTS

It's a . . . Brushbot!

"Should we just . . . start?" Bella Diaz asked, glancing at her watch.

"Let's wait a few more minutes," Emily Adams suggested.

"Yeah," agreed Maddie Wilson.

The three friends were at their craft clubhouse—formerly known as the old shed in Bella's backyard. Usually, it was *four* friends, but Sam Sharma was nowhere in sight.

The craft clubhouse was filled with all sorts of materials the kids used for their crafty projects. They had a Sewing Station, where Maddie could often be found. There was a Coding Corner, with a computer that Bella had installed. Emily's Carpentry Cabinet contained

tons of tools, gadgets, and materials like nuts and bolts. And Sam's Painting Pavilion housed different color paints and about a million brushes of different sizes.

But where *was* Sam?

"Sorry I am late!" someone shouted as the shed door flew open. *There* was Sam, breathless. "I had to clean my hamster's cage. It takes forever!" he explained.

Maddie nodded sympathetically. "I know what that's like," she said.

"I mean, having to do chores. It's my job to set the dinner table *every* night!"

"You're both lucky," said Bella. "Since my dad is a chef, he uses every pot and pan when he cooks. And guess who has to clean up? *But* the other night, doing the dishes actually gave me an amazing idea for a new crafting project. Behold!"

Bella handed an object to each of her friends.

"Scrub brushes?" asked Sam, confused.

"Right now, yes," said Bella. "But we're going to transform them into: Brushbots!"

Bella opened her notebook to a diagram. "A Brushbot is a battery-powered scrub brush that can move on its own," she explained.

"And sort of looks like a robot! That's genius!" exclaimed Sam.

The first step was for each of them to attach a battery pack to a scrub brush. The kids continued working, carefully following Bella's instructions.

"Before we decorate them, let's try them out!" Bella suggested. "On the count of three. One, two . . ."

"THREE!" everyone yelled, flipping the switches.

Nothing happened.

"What did we do wrong?" Maddie asked.

"Maybe these batteries are duds?" suggested Emily.

Bella looked concerned. "But they're brand-new," she said.

"Are they the *right* kind of batteries?" asked Sam.

Bella pulled out a battery and examined it. Then she started to

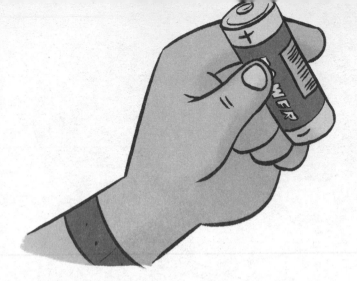

laugh. "I think I know what went wrong. You see how each battery has a plus sign at one end and a minus at the other?"

The other three nodded.

"Well, to make the connection, positive and negative need to be in the right positions. Once we do that . . ."

The friends rotated the batteries and flipped the switches. The Brushbots started working immediately!

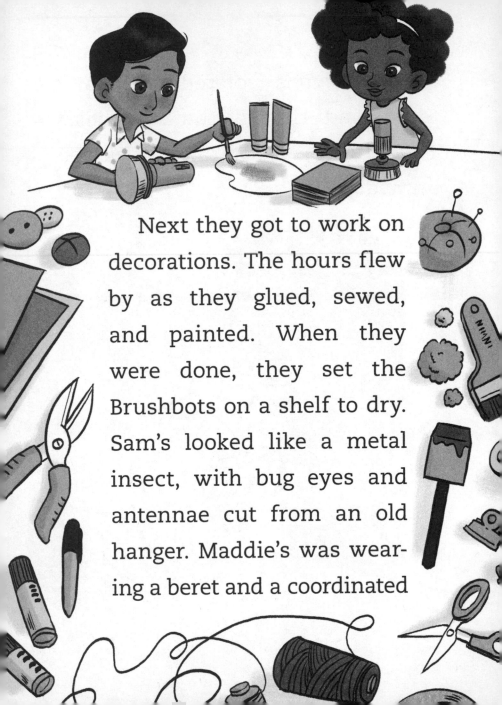

Next they got to work on decorations. The hours flew by as they glued, sewed, and painted. When they were done, they set the Brushbots on a shelf to dry. Sam's looked like a metal insect, with bug eyes and antennae cut from an old hanger. Maddie's was wearing a beret and a coordinated outfit. Emily's had nuts and bolts glued on in cool patterns. And Bella's looked like a real robot, with electric wires wrapping around in all different directions.

"Bring on the dirty dishes!" said Bella.

Maddie laughed. "I think I like mine too much to use it for chores!" she admitted.

Emily and Sam nodded in agreement.

"You guys!" said Bella, though she knew her friends were right. Her Brushbot *had* turned out really cool too.

Looked like she'd have to keep doing the dinner dishes the old-fashioned way . . . for now.

What's *Your* Talent?

At school the next day, the kids gathered for the Monday-morning assembly. Onstage, their principal, Ms. Park, began announcements.

"I have some exciting news!" she said. "Mason Creek Elementary will be hosting a school-wide talent show. Students can participate on their own or in groups."

Bella, Emily, Maddie, and Sam exchanged knowing looks. Sure, they would need to figure out what to do, but even without discussing it they knew they would work on their act together.

Principal Park continued, saying, "You can perform a song or a dance, read a story or a poem, juggle, or even help out backstage. This is an exciting event that will showcase the talents of our entire school community!"

At recess, the four friends gathered on the playground.

"What should we do for the talent show?" asked Maddie.

"Not singing, please," said Bella. "I don't even sound good when I sing in the shower," she added with a sheepish smile.

"Not dancing, either," said Emily. "My fancy footwork is strictly for the soccer field."

"I'm going to twirl my baton," their classmate Joelle said, marching by and flipping her baton into the air to demonstrate.

"I'm going to do magic," pro-claimed Lyle, another classmate. He pulled out a deck of cards and fanned them in front of the friends.

"And I'll be his magician's assis-tant!" said Lyle's best friend, Cory.

Alana and Kai, two other classmates, came running up. "Maddie!"
said Alana. "We're going to write a
play for the talent show. Would you
do the costumes?"

Maddie was really flattered. "I'm sorry!" she said. "But I already have a group."

"That's okay! What are you guys doing?" asked Kai.

The four friends looked at each other.

"Well . . . we're not sure yet," Sam finally answered.

Kai frowned, then brightened up. "I'm sure it will be something great!" she said enthusiastically.

The school bell rang just then, and Kai and Alana hurried off.

"So . . . meet at the craft clubhouse after school?" Bella asked.

The other three kids couldn't have said "Yes!" faster.

Out of Ideas

That afternoon at Bella's house, the four friends grabbed their go-to snack—lemonade and a big bowl of popcorn with Bella's dad's special spice blend on it—and trooped out to the craft clubhouse.

"Brainstorming time!" Maddie said. "And just remember, like Ms. Gibbons always says . . ."

"'When you brainstorm, there are no bad ideas,'" everyone said together, repeating one of their teacher's favorite sayings.

"I'll make a list," offered Sam.

"No singing," Bella reminded him.

"And no dancing," added Emily.

"So far this is a list of things we're *not* doing," Sam pointed out.

Bella sighed. "Well, we can't exactly code a computer game onstage," she said.

Emily nodded in agreement. "Or build a tree house," she added.

"Guys, I hear you," said Maddie patiently. "But let's keep thinking. I'm sure something great will come to us. Like, we could do a fashion show."

"Or paint something together," suggested Sam. "I'm not sure *how*, but I'm going to write it down anyway." He added his idea and Maddie's to the list.

"Hmm . . . we could build a robot and show how it works onstage?" Bella said.

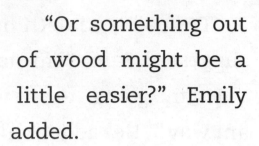

"Or something out of wood might be a little easier?" Emily added.

"This is a good start," said Sam, after adding both ideas. "My dad will be here soon to take me to my art class, so here's our list so far. Add more ideas if you think of any, okay?"

He pinned the list to the clubhouse wall and then left to meet his dad.

The girls crowded around to take a look.

Finally, Emily spoke. She said what everyone was thinking: "There aren't any *bad* ideas here. But I'm not sure there are any *great* ideas yet, either."

CHAPTER
4

Inspiration Strikes!

When Sam got home after art class, dinner was almost ready. His little sister, Yasmin, was at the table drawing.

"Hi, Mom! Hi, Yazzy!" called Sam. He hung up his backpack and kicked off his sneakers.

Sam quickly set the table and gave Yasmin a piece of naan to

nibble so she wouldn't complain when he swapped her paper and crayons for a place mat and dishes.

"Such a busy day at work today!" said Sam's mom, who was a high-school art teacher. She carried a steaming bowl of chana masala to the table. Sam's mouth watered. Usually he didn't like chickpeas. But somehow his mom made them delicious!

"You should have been an architect instead of a teacher," teased his dad. "Much less stressful."

"Oh, really? What about that time you cut your finger building that model of the museum?"

Sam's parents laughed.

"When you guys were in school together," said Sam, "did you ever have to do a talent show?"

"Sure," said his dad. "At our

school talent show, I got everyone on their feet with my rock and roll."

"You did?" Sam was impressed.

"Kind of," admitted Sam's dad. "Mostly because they got up to use the bathroom when I played. I was pretty bad. Your mom's the real musician."

"You played rock music?" Sam asked his mom.

She smiled. "Classical guitar and jazz."

"I really want to find something I can do with my friends," Sam said. "We tried to figure it out today, but we just don't have any good ideas."

"Give it time," said Sam's mother gently.

"Inspiration can strike when you least expect it," added his dad.

Sam waited for inspiration to strike all through dinner. He waited for it as he helped clear the table.

He waited for it through his science homework, then math.

Stumped by a division problem, Sam began tapping his pencil. *Come on, inspiration. Where are you?* he thought.

"You about ready to call it a night, Sam?"

Sam looked up and saw his dad standing in the doorway. "Oh. Uh, sure. Just a few more math problems."

"Okay," said his dad. "Nice beat."

"Beat?" Sam looked down and realized that he was still tapping his pencil against the desk.

"Sounds good. You're already a better drummer than I was a guitar player," his dad said.

Sam grinned. Then, all of a sudden, an idea hit him. If he could make a drum out of a pencil and a desk, maybe he and his friends could create other instruments too! Then they could perform a song

while showcasing their crafting talents. And they wouldn't have to sing or dance!

Sam tried to turn his attention back to math, but he kept tapping his pencil excitedly. He couldn't wait to tell his friends!

Cereal Boxes
and Jingle Bells

At school the next day, Sam shared his idea.

"I love it!" said Emily.

"Ooh, and we'll need something cool to wear as a band," said Maddie. "I'm on it!"

"Awesome!" said Bella. "What instruments should we make?"

Just then their teacher walked in.

"Come along, everyone," said Ms. Gibbons. "We have music first today."

"Perfect!" whispered Bella as the kids lined up. "Now we can look at everything in the music room

and figure out what instruments to make."

The suggestion sounded simple enough. But there were so many different instruments in the music room: triangles, drums, guitars, shakers, tambourines, and more! The four friends all took note of the instruments and how they might re-create them. They didn't have a chance to talk about their ideas for the rest of the day, so they were all excited to meet up at Bella's house later.

"We'll definitely need a guitar," said Bella, putting some home-made cookies on a plate for them to take out to the clubhouse. "I took lessons, so I know how to play. I just have to figure out how to make one."

Sam picked up a wooden spoon from the counter and pretended to play it like a guitar.

"Hey, wait a second!" Emily took the spoon and positioned it by a box of cereal that was nearby. The spoon formed the long neck of the guitar and the box formed its body.

"Awesome!" said Bella. Then she went over to the kitchen recycling bin. "What if instead of the spoon we used this?" She pulled out a long box that had once held spaghetti.

"Oh, and look!" Maddie reached into the recycling bin and pulled out two oatmeal containers. "What could we use these for?"

"Drums!" said Sam instantly.

They carried their cookies and found materials out to the craft clubhouse and got to work. Maddie was still excited about the idea of band outfits, so she dug through the boxes of sewing supplies in search of just the right things.

"What about these?" she asked, pulling out a bag of shiny silver balls.

"Jingle bells?" asked Emily. "Won't we look a little silly, like jesters or elves, if we wear those?"

Maddie laughed. "Not for our out-fits," she said. "For an instrument!"

"Ohhhh!" Emily took the bag and shook it. "Right! These remind me of the bell shakers in the music room!"

Emily grabbed two long wooden dowels. "I can drill holes and attach the bells!" she said excitedly.

She took the supplies over to the woodworking bench and put on her safety goggles.

"I guess that just leaves me," said Maddie.

Bella looked up from her work. "There are lots of things you can make, Maddie. You're so talented!"

"I'm sure something will come to you," added Sam. "Inspiration can strike when you least expect it!"

"You guys are probably right," said Maddie. "I'll just keep working on our outfits until I think of something. It would be *terrible* if we didn't look as great as we sounded!"

A Leaky Disaster

By Friday the friends had created an amazing assortment of instruments. Bella had built a guitar out of a cereal box and two pasta boxes. It had rubber-band strings and cork knobs. It also had paperclip frets, so it actually could be played! Sam had a complete oatmeal-canister drum set, plus cymbals made out of paper

plates. In typical Sam fashion, he had painted the drum set with all sorts of patterns and designs in every color imaginable. Emily had made several percussion pieces, including her bell shakers and shakers made out of paper cups filled with dried beans.

"We're going to rock!" said Sam, and the others cheered in agreement.

The only band member who was still instrumentless was Maddie. She kept busy sewing while waiting for inspiration to strike.

On Saturday morning Bella woke up early. She looked outside and noticed that the grass was wet. Really wet. The sun was shining, but it looked like it had probably rained all night.

I'll go see if the glue on my guitar is dry, she thought.

She slipped on her rain boots and sloshed out to the clubhouse. She flung open the door and—

"Oh no!" she cried.

The clubhouse was . . . a disaster. It seemed that the roof had leaked overnight during the rainstorm.

Almost everything in the shed was completely drenched! And that included all their instruments. Bella's guitar was a soggy mess, as were Sam's drums. Emily's noise-makers had fared a little bit better, but not by much. Luckily, Bella's beloved computer seemed fine.

A little while later the other three kids arrived at the clubhouse.

They all gasped when they saw the damage.

"What are we going to do?" asked Bella.

"Well, I say we start by cleaning up," said Emily.

The others agreed. They got to work inspecting the contents of the clubhouse. They threw out what was

damaged and set other things out to dry in the sun. Emily grabbed a ladder and a flashlight and climbed up to examine the roof.

"Be careful!" said Bella. "It's probably slippery up there."

"I don't have to actually go on the roof," Emily reassured her. "I just need to stand on the ladder so I can reach the spot that needs patching."

"I'll help you," offered Maddie. She held the ladder steady, handed up tools, and accepted items that Emily handed down. Emily passed

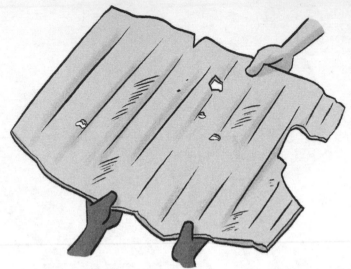

down a big square of corrugated metal that was filled with holes. Clearly *that* was the cause of the leak.

Throughout the morning, the team worked hard on cleaning and repairs. At lunchtime Bella's father brought out a tray of sandwiches, plus tortilla chips and delicious homemade salsa. He also brought something else.

"A can of coffee?" Bella looked confused.

"It's empty," her father said. "I thought it might make a good metal drum? You know, a waterproof one."

"Awesome!" said Sam. "Do you have any other waterproof cans?"

Bella's dad smiled. "Of course! I'm a chef, remember? I have tomato cans, jalapeño pepper cans, and olive oil drums, plus huge plastic containers from the restaurant supply store."

Sam followed Mr. Diaz to the kitchen. When he returned, his arms were full. "These are going

to be even *better* drums than the ones I made before!" he exclaimed.

Seeing Sam with the metal cans, Maddie suddenly had an idea.

"Mr. Diaz?" she asked. "Can I have the piece of metal that came off the roof?"

"What for?" asked Bella.

"Oh, you'll see," said Maddie mysteriously.

CHAPTER

7

Starting All Over

The next week was a busy one as the four friends struggled to repair and replace their damaged instruments. Bella was pleased to find a jumbo-size cereal box in the recycling bin, which made a better guitar body. She found more pasta boxes too. However, she ran into a new problem.

Boing! Boing!

"Ow!" said Sam. A rubber band had popped off Bella's guitar and flown across the room, striking him on the elbow.

"Sorry!" said Bella. *Twang!* Another rubber band broke off her guitar. "I don't know if I can make this work. These rubber bands keep popping off or breaking."

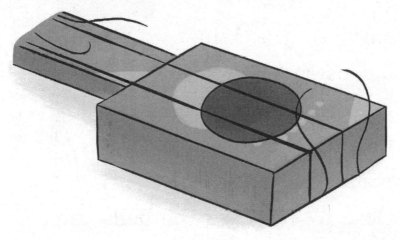

"Have you tried using bigger ones?" asked Sam. "I can bring some in tomorrow. My dad has a whole bunch for rolling up his architectural drawings."

"That would be great!"

"Meanwhile," said Emily, "some of my shakers survived the rain, but listen." She shook her bell shakers while the others listened. "I made the holes too close together, so the bells can't jingle. Guess I'm going to have to start over after all."

"I'm actually glad I had to make new drums," said Sam. "Check this out." He hit his drums in turn.

"They each have a different sound," observed Emily.

"I know," said Sam. "Before, they sounded the same because they were the same material. But these are different sizes and different materials. So now the beats make all sorts of sounds!"

"Maddie, when are you going to show us what *your* instrument is?" asked Bella.

Maddie was hunched over something, her back to her friends. They could see that she was tying a bow around the back of her neck.

"Now!" she said as she turned around.

Maddie was *wearing* the piece of corrugated metal that had come off the roof as if it were a long bib. It hung from a ribbon around her neck. She was holding a metal soup spoon and a wire whisk, which she

proceeded to scrape up and down the zigzag surface of the metal, producing a really cool scratchy sound.

"Wow," said Sam. "What is it?"

"It's called a zydeco washboard," announced Maddie. "My uncle Alvin lives in New Orleans. He plays one

in a band. Emily helped me trim the sides and bend the top edge so it sits right on my shoulders."

"I can't believe it, but our instruments are even better than before!" said Bella. "I guess we have the rain to thank."

"Rain, hard work, patience, and the best friends ever," said Maddie, whisking her washboard with a flourish.

"I think it's about time we start practicing!" suggested Emily.

After all, the talent show was in three days!

CHAPTER
8

Practice, Practice, Practice!

The next day the band members gathered at the Craft Clubhouse, ready to practice.

"Okay, why don't we start with a simple song?" said Bella.

"How about 'Twinkle, Twinkle, Little Star'?" suggested Emily.

"Sure!" said Bella. And she started strumming her guitar. "And

a one, and a two, and a three, let's go!"

Emily joined in using her shakers and bells. Sam picked up the beat on his drums. And Maddie whisked along on her washboard.

When they got to the end of the song, the friends looked at each other.

"Not bad," said Bella.

"But not *great*," said Emily.

The friends tried a few other songs, but none of them were quite right. Then Bella had an idea.

"Maybe," she said, "we should play something different. Like . . . our own song?"

"How would we do that?" asked Sam.

"Well, in my guitar lessons, we used to improvise sometimes," Bella said. "Like this: Sam, drop a beat."

Sam began tapping out a rhythm on his drums.

"Now I'm going to add my guitar." Bella began strumming, paying attention to Sam's beat but weaving in her own twangy notes.

"Maddie, you ready to jump in?" Bella asked.

Maddie nodded and began skritch-scratching away.

"Guessing that means it's my turn," said Emily, and she picked up two shakers so she could add two distinct sounds to the song they were forming.

Slowly, smiles came to all four faces.

"We sound . . . not bad!" said Bella. The others nodded in agreement.

"If we keep practicing, we're going to sound great!" said Sam.

And so they practiced for the rest of the afternoon.

By the time Maddie's, Emily's, and Sam's parents came to pick them up, the kids were exhausted.

As Maddie was walking out, she suddenly gasped and turned around. "Guys, we don't have a band name!"

CHAPTER 9

Four Surprises

The day before the talent show, all of Mason Creek Elementary was buzzing with excitement.

To Emily, Maddie, Bella, and Sam, it felt like the longest school day ever. Finally the bell rang. The four friends grabbed their things and practically ran out of the school building.

"Hey, what's that?" asked Emily, noticing Maddie was carrying an extra bag.

"It's a surprise," said Maddie mysteriously.

And when they all arrived at the craft studio, Maddie showed her friends what exactly was in that bag.

She pulled out four black T-shirts. Each one had a band member's name scrawled on the back in silver fabric paint. Maddie had then decorated the backs with patches and buttons and designs out of multicolored threads. Each one was unique.

"These are so cool!" Emily exclaimed.

"But there's one thing missing," said Maddie. "There's nothing on the front of the shirts because we haven't picked a band name yet!"

"Fantastic Four?" threw out Sam.

"*Craftastic* Four?" Bella chimed in.

"What about Craftastic *Crew*?" Emily suggested.

At that suggestion, a smile spread across the face of each kid. That was it!

Maddie had brought her silver paint with her. She grabbed brushes from Sam's Painting Pavilion and passed them around so everyone could add their new band name to the custom T-shirts.

"Hey, speaking of painting, I have a surprise too." Sam pulled out a roll of paper from a long tube he had borrowed from his dad. He unrolled it to display a gorgeous painted backdrop for the band.

"That's amazing, Sam!" said Emily.

"I left room for the band name," Sam pointed out. "And I think I have some regular silver paint that would match the T-shirts perfectly!"

"I *also* have a surprise," said Emily. She went to the back of the shed and pulled out a wooden storage crate to which she had added

wheels and a handle. "This way we can bring our instruments into the auditorium more easily."

"And I borrowed some extra microphones from the music room, plus speakers to rig them up to," said Bella.

"Wow," said Sam, admiring the shirts, the instruments, and the gear. "We make a pretty great team, don't we?"

And it was true. They really did make a good team. But that team also knew they needed just a little more practice.

Following Bella's lead, the kids picked up their instruments and got in position. The talent show was the next night, so it was their last chance to get their sound just right!

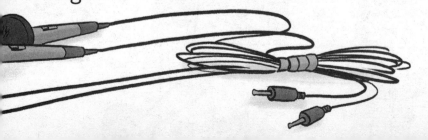

CHAPTER 10

Rock On!

"Good evening! Welcome to the Mason Creek Elementary School talent show."

Principal Park stood at the microphone, beaming. Bella, Maddie, Emily, and Sam waited backstage. They were surrounded by jugglers, gymnasts, singers, dancers, and other talented classmates.

Sam tapped his drumsticks nervously. He could hear the audience clapping and laughing as Lyle and Cory did their infamous pulling-a-frog-out-of-a-hat magic trick onstage.

"We're next," said Bella.

Suddenly Maddie gasped. "Where are my whisk and spoon?" she asked frantically.

Everyone searched about, but they were nowhere to be found.

"What am I going to do?" Maddie knew her washboard would work only if she had something to play it with. Meanwhile, the magic act was about to end and they would be going onstage soon! Maddie was close to tears. All that hard work only to have it ruined by a last-minute mix-up.

Bella, who had been digging through her backpack, pulled out two objects and held them out to Maddie. "Try using these instead!"

"Really?" asked Maddie.

Bella shrugged. "What do you have to lose?"

Before Maddie could reply, Lyle and Cory returned triumphantly and the friends heard Principal Park introducing the next act.

"I'm proud to introduce four students who are so creative, they don't just make music. They make their own musical instruments, too! I present to you: the Craftastic Crew."

The big moment had arrived. The four friends marched onstage and set up their instruments.

Sam looked at the others, gave a nod, and began to tap out a beat on his drums.

Tap, tap, tap-tap-tap.

Bella joined in, twanging away at her strings. Emily came in next, adding the rhythm of her various shakers to the mix.

Maddie took a deep breath. "Here goes nothing," she whispered. Then she took the two Brushbots Bella had handed to her and scratched their stiff bristles tentatively across her washboard.

Scritcha-scritcha! Scritcha-scritcha!

The scratchy noise was perfect! Encouraged, she flipped the switches and the Brushbots sprang to life, scrubbing away. She moved them up and down on her washboard, producing a faster scratching sound than before, which sounded great.

Then the audience started clapping along!

It's like a real jam session, thought Sam, drumming away excitedly.

The audience really likes our sound, thought Bella. She closed her eyes and imagined herself rocking out in a huge stadium.

When they finished playing,
there was a brief moment of silence.
Then thunderous applause!

The friends could not stop grinning even after they were backstage.

"We did it!" said Bella, jumping up and down.

That night, even though it had been a long and exhausting day, Bella couldn't seem to fall asleep. She picked up her homemade guitar and plucked its strings, remembering how it felt to perform in front of the whole school with her best friends. It was funny how they'd started with nothing, not even an idea. Then they'd lost everything to a leaky roof. But they didn't give up. They had worked together and—Bella stood on her bed, strummed a chord, and struck a pose—the Craftastic Crew had totally *rocked* the talent show!

How to Make . . .
A Cereal Box Guitar

What you need:

Cereal box
Spaghetti box
Craft knife
Rubber bands

Glue
Corks
Straw
Paints and paintbrush

Step 1:

Paint the boxes
any way you like!

Cut out a circle from one side of the cereal box.

Stretch the rubber bands over the middle of the cereal box.

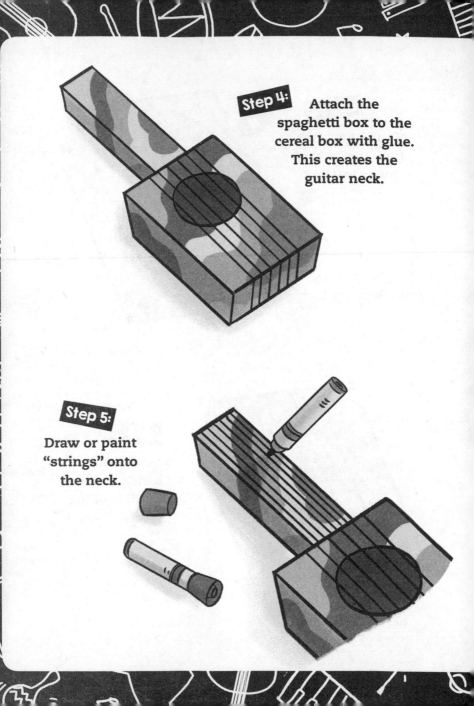

Step 4: Attach the spaghetti box to the cereal box with glue. This creates the guitar neck.

Step 5:

Draw or paint "strings" onto the neck.

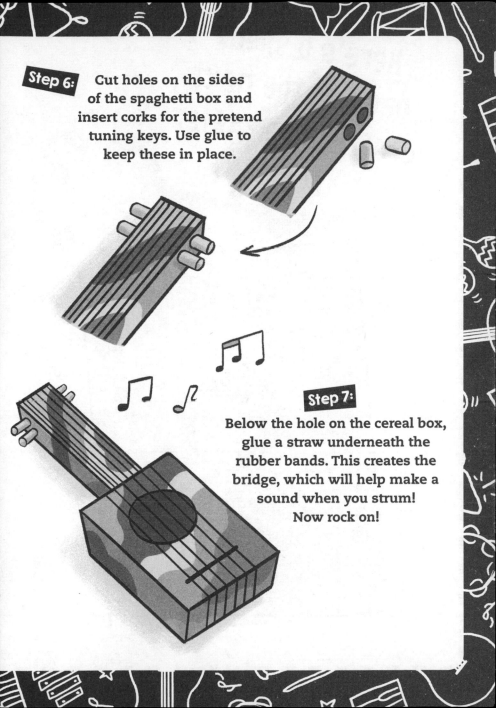

Step 6: Cut holes on the sides of the spaghetti box and insert corks for the pretend tuning keys. Use glue to keep these in place.

Step 7: Below the hole on the cereal box, glue a straw underneath the rubber bands. This creates the bridge, which will help make a sound when you strum! Now rock on!

Here's a sneak peek at the next Craftily Ever After book!

Craftily EVER AFTER

--Tie-Dye Disaster--

by Martha Maker

illustrated by Xindi Yan

Maddie was just adding the final touches to her latest design sketch when a familiar, mouthwatering smell reached her. "*Mmmmmmm!* Dad's pancakes!"

When she finished eating, she visited her mom in her sewing studio.

"Hi, sweetie," said Margie Wilson, looking up from her sewing machine. "Do you have time to give me some feedback on my designs? I need someone with a critical eye and a passion for fashion."

"Sure!" said Maddie. It was fun to have a mom who was a seamstress. Maddie thoughtfully studied several pencil sketches with swatches of fabric taped to them. "Hmmm . . . that dress would look amazing if you added some sequins to the hemline. And maybe using a brighter color, like coral, would make it pop—"

Just then Maddie's dad burst in, holding out a phone.

"It's him!" he whispered urgently.